USBORNE
Lift-the-flap
ON THE BEACH

Alastair Smith and Laura Howell
Illustrated by Ian Jackson
Designed by Candice Whatmore and Karen Tomlins

Digital imaging by Keith Furnival

On the seashore

The seashore is where the sea meets the land. This seashore is a sandy beach.

Sand is made from tiny pieces of rock and shells. Damp sand is good for making sandcastles.

Tip the bucket over to see what's inside.

These seagulls
are looking
for food.

This one has found
something tasty.
Lucky seagull!

Shells and pebbles

Some little seaside animals have shells. The shells keep them safe from rough waves and hungry birds.

The sea rubs pebbles together and makes them smooth.

What's under this empty shell?

This wood has been battered by the sea. The salty water turned it white.

Oyster shells open and close like a book.

Hermit crabs live in the shells of animals that died. As they grow, they move to a bigger shell.

A rock pool

Here's a little pool in the rocks on the seashore. It's full of sea water. Little creatures live and hide in the pool.

What can you find in this rock pool?

There's lots of slimy, slippy seaweed here. Watch out when you stand on it.

These red blobs are animals called sea anemones.

The pale yellow shells are limpets.

The blue shells are mussels.

Crabs

A crab has a hard shell and two strong claws.

My claws are stronger than your hands.

Watch out! A crab can give you a nasty pinch with its claws.

Can you find any more crabs? They sometimes hide under stones.

As a crab grows, its shell splits and falls off. Then it grows a new one.

You might find empty crab shells like this on the seashore.

Under the sea

Lots of plants and
animals live in
the shallow water
near the seashore.

Can you find
some tiny fish?

Little shelled
animals cling
to rocks so
they don't get
washed away.

The seaweed grips
the rocks, too.

These are jellyfish.
Their soft bodies are
shaped like umbrellas.

Look at how
the sun shines
down through
the water.

Who's hiding
behind this
rock?

Ships and boats

Every day the sea comes in and goes out again. The boats are tied up to stop them from floating away.

The green boat is tied to a buoy.

Can you see what the red boat is tied to?

Buoy

Here is a fishing boat. It has caught a lot of fish.

The seagulls are off to grab some fish from the boat.

Fishing boats have big nets, like these. They catch lots of fish very quickly.

Rocky cliffs

This lighthouse sits on the rocky shore. A bright light shines from it.

The light warns ships not to sail near the rocks.

At night, when it is dark, the light can be seen from far, far away.

Waves batter the land and wear it away. This is how the cliffs are made.

Long ago, these rocky stumps were part of the cliffs. Now look at them!

Lots of birds make their nests high up on the rocky cliffs.

These birds are gannets. They dive into the sea and grab fish to eat.

This is a puffin. She has caught some fish for her chick to eat.

Can you find the puffin's chick?

This book has shown you some of the
exciting things that you can find by the sea.
Next time you're on the beach, why not
see what else you can discover?

This new, enlarged edition first published in 2004 by Usborne Publishing Ltd, Usborne House,
83-85 Saffron Hill, London EC1N 8RT, England.
www.usborne.com
Copyright © Usborne Publishing Ltd, 2004, 2002.

Printed in China.